BEHIND THE SCENES
BIOGRAPHIES

WHAT YOU NEVER KNEW ABOUT

JENNA ORTEGA

by Helen Cox Cannons

CAPSTONE PRESS
a capstone imprint

Published by Spark, an imprint of Capstone
1710 Roe Crest Drive, North Mankato, Minnesota 56003
capstonepub.com

Library of Congress Cataloging-in-Publication Data is available
on the Library of Congress website.
ISBN: 9781669072898 (hardcover)
ISBN: 9781669073024 (paperback)
ISBN: 9781669072935 (ebook PDF)

Summary: Jenna Ortega started acting at 9 years old. But what commercials
did she star in as a child? How many siblings does she have? From TV to fashion,
Jenna Ortega is a mogul in the making.

Editorial Credits
Editor: Christianne Jones; Designer: Elijah Blue; Media Researcher: Jo Miller;
Production Specialist: Whitney Schaefer

Image Credits
Alamy: FlixPix, 13, 22, ZUMA Press, Inc., 17; Getty Images: Amy Sussman, 4, Bruce
Glikas, 18, Dia Dipasupil, 9, Dimitrios Kambouris, 27, Emma McIntyre, 23, Jerod Harris,
15, Phillip Faraone, cover, Rachel Murray, 20 Tasos Katopodis, 29; Shutterstock: Anton
Vierietin, 24 (middle), Elena Pimukova, 16, Evan El-Amin, 14, Inspired Vectorizator, 8,
Janet Delight, 28, Kathy Hutchins, 7, 11, 21, 25, Martial Red, 6, Mega Pixel, 10,
Nynke van Holten, 24 (left), Scorpp, 24 (right), the8monkey, 24 (top)

Design Elements: Shutterstock: Chief Design, cuppuccino, IIIerlok_xolms

Printed in the United States   6156

TABLE OF CONTENTS

Words in **bold** are in the glossary.

LEADING **LADY**

She was a Disney darling. Now she's a leading lady! Jenna Ortega started acting at 9 years old. Now she is one of the hottest actors in Hollywood. With her talent, it's easy to see why.

What else is there to know about Jenna? Read on to find out!

JENNA'S **FAVES**

How much do you really know about Jenna? Test your knowledge!

1. **Favorite Disney movie?**

2. **Favorite food?**

3. **Favorite emoji?**

4. **Favorite pizza topping?**

5. **Favorite season?**

FACT

Jenna is a talented soccer player. She was part of the American Youth Soccer Organization.

1. The Lion King **2.** chocolate cake **3.** winking face with tongue out **4.** jalapeño **5.** summer

What does Jenna do when she's not acting? She likes to write. It's her favorite hobby. In fact, she's a **published** author. Her first book, *It's All Love: Reflections for Your Heart & Soul,* came out in 2021.

FROM **BURGERS** **TO** HOLLYWOOD

Jenna was discovered when she was 7 years old. Her mom shared a video of her on Facebook. What was Jenna's first job? It was a toothpaste commercial. She was also in three McDonald's commercials in one year.

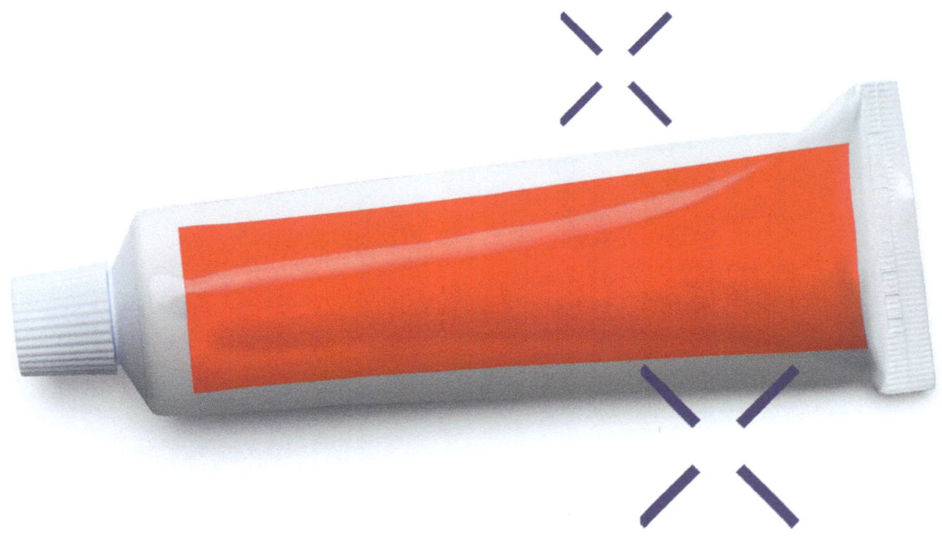

Jenna has acted in lots of shows and movies. She is best known for her role as Wednesday Addams on the TV show *Wednesday*.

As Wednesday, Jenna did a solo dance routine. It went **viral**. Jenna made up the dance herself. She felt unsure about doing it. But her co-stars told her to go for it.

> **FACT**
> Jenna learned to play the cello for her role as Wednesday.

FIRST FEMALE PRESIDENT?

Barack Obama was a huge inspiration for Jenna. When Jenna said she wanted to be an actor, her mom didn't believe her. Why? Because Jenna had wanted to be the first female president just a week earlier.

"To this day, I'm still obsessed with Obama."

—Jenna, *Elle* interview, 2023

STUCK IN THE MIDDLE

Stuck in the Middle was a hit show for Disney. It was a hit part for Jenna too. She played Harley Diaz, the middle child in a big family. This was not hard for Jenna to imagine. She has five siblings and is a middle child.

MUSIC AWARDS
Disney CHANNEL
Goldfish FLAVOR BLASTED
Macaroni & Cheese Shapes
CHRYSLER
Disney CHANNEL
xfinity
American Girl
Goldfish FLAVOR BLASTED
Disney CHANNEL
beads
Disney CHANNEL

HOLLYWOOD
DJ
KIDS FASHION

Jenna's parents are very supportive. However, they aren't interested in the Hollywood lifestyle. Famous or not, Jenna had to do chores growing up. If she didn't do them, the chores multiplied.

FACT

Isaac, Mariah, Mia, and twins Aaliyah and Markus are Jenna's siblings.

PALS AND
PUPPIES

From left: Jenna Ortega, Landry Bender, Madison Hu, Olivia Rodrigo

Jenna is close friends with Olivia Rodrigo. They met on the set of the Disney show *Bizaardvark* in 2018.

Olivia Rodrigo

"Jenna and I grew up together on the Disney Channel, which is a very strange way to grow up."
—Olivia Rodrigo, 2023

Jenna is great friends with her *Wednesday* co-star, Emma Myers. Emma played Wednesday's roommate, Enid Sinclair. They filmed the show in Romania and spent lots of time together.

Jenna loves her dogs. She has three. One is a Labradoodle named Kylo. She got Kylo in 2017 as a Christmas present. Jenna also has a Maltipoo named Anna and a Yorkshire terrier named Brooklyn.

Maltipoo

Labradoodle

Yorkshire terrier

STYLE QUEEN

Fashion is a big part of Jenna's life. She was in her first fashion **campaign** in 2021.

Jenna's style has changed as she has gotten older. In her younger days, Jenna had a sweet look. Now Jenna wears Wednesday's trademark bangs. She is also more adventurous in her fashion choices.

LATINA LEGACY

Jenna is of Mexican and Puerto Rican **heritage**. She is very proud of her background. She was the voice of Isabel on *Elena of Avalor*. Elena was the first Disney Latina princess. Isabel was her little sister.

FACT
Jenna's family eats tamales every Christmas.

"... A Latina princess was long overdue, and to be able to play one is a dream come true."

—Jenna, *People en Español*

Glossary

campaign (kam-PEYN)—organized actions and events with a specific goal

heritage (HER-uh-tij)—the culture and traditions of one's family, ancestors, or country

publish (PUH-blish)—to produce and distribute a book, magazine, newspaper, or any other printed material for sale

viral (VYE-ruhl)—something that spreads quickly by social media and reaches thousands or millions of people in a short time

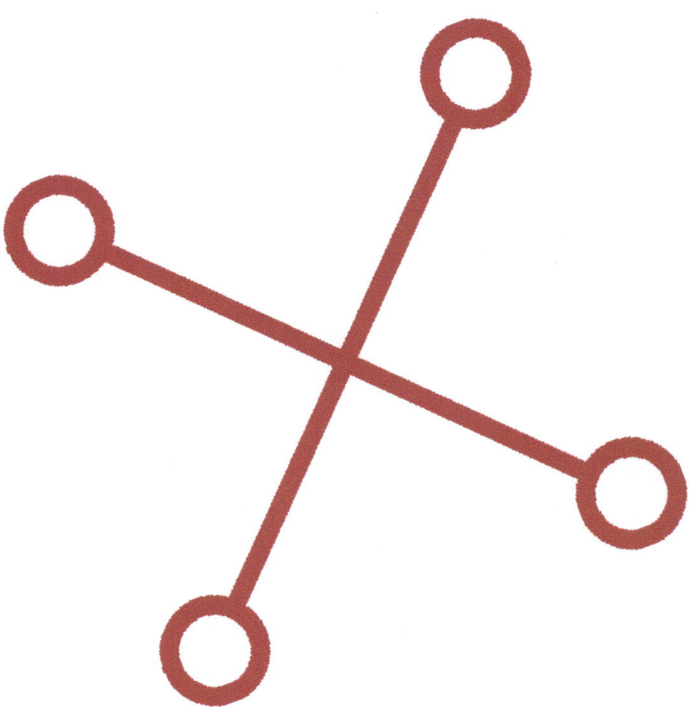

Read More

Allen, Nafeesah. *What You Never Knew About Olivia Rodrigo.* Mankato, MN: Capstone Publishing, 2023.

Ortega, Jenna. *It's All Love: Reflections for Your Heart & Soul.* New York: Random House, 2021.

Vourvoulias, Sabrina. *Nuestra America: 30 Inspiring Latinas/Latinos Who Have Shaped the United States.* New York: Running Press Kids, 2020.

Internet Sites

Britannica: Jenna Ortega
britannica.com/biography/Jenna-Ortega

Jenna Ortega World
jenna-ortega.com

Kiddle: Jenna Ortega Facts for Kids
kids.kiddle.co/Jenna_Ortega

Index

About the Author

Helen Cox Cannons was born in Dumfriesshire, Scotland. She has a Master's Degree in English Literature from the University of Edinburgh. She has worked as an editor and author for more than 25 years. Helen likes to crochet, sing, go for country walks, and fuss over her two cats, Nero and Diego, and trusty hound, Alba. She now lives in Oxfordshire with her two daughters, Abby and Serena.